Dear Parent:
Your child's love of reading starts here!

Every child learns to read in a different way and at his or her own speed. Some go back and forth between reading levels and read favorite books again and again. Others read through each level in order. You can help your young reader improve and become more confident by encouraging his or her own interests and abilities. From books your child reads with you to the first books he or she reads alone, there are I Can Read Books for every stage of reading:

SHARED READING
Basic language, word repetition, and whimsical illustrations, ideal for sharing with your emergent reader

BEGINNING READING
Short sentences, familiar words, and simple concepts for children eager to read on th

D0971460

READING WITH HELP
Engaging stories, longer sentences, and language play for developing readers

READING ALONE
Complex plots, challenging vocabulary, and high-interest topics for the independent reader

I Can Read Books have introduced children to the joy of reading since 1957. Featuring award-winning authors and illustrators and a fabulous cast of beloved characters, I Can Read Books set the standard for beginning readers.

A lifetime of discovery begins with the magical words "I Can Read!"

Visit www.icanread.com for information
on enriching your child's reading experience.

To our kids and our fur babies,
for the loves, laughs, and messes
—*K. D. & S. R. J.*

For my little brother Tre,
and all the fun times we had trying to make
that perfect cupcake when we were kids
—*J. M.*

The full-color artwork was created digitally.

I Can Read® and I Can Read Book® are trademarks of HarperCollins Publishers.

Library of Congress Control Number: 2020947133
ISBN 978-0-06-294612-6 (hardcover) — ISBN 978-0-06-294611-9 (paperback)

21 22 23 24 25   CWM   10 9 8 7 6 5   ❖   First Edition
                              📖 Greenwillow Books

READING 3 ALONE

I Can Read!

Libby
LOVES SCIENCE

Mix and Measure

By KIMBERLY DERTING
and SHELLI R. JOHANNES
pictures by JOELLE MURRAY

Greenwillow Books
An Imprint of HarperCollins Publishers

On Saturday morning, Libby got up early.

She fed her dog, Sprinkles.

Then she made her own breakfast.

Today was a special day.

"Happy birthday, Sprinkles!"

Libby said, hugging her dog.

"What time is the Puppy Party?"
asked Libby's mother.

"It starts in two hours," Libby said.

"Rosa is coming over now
to help me get ready."

"I want to help, too," said Leo,
Libby's little brother.

As soon as Rosa arrived, they got started.

"We need some doggie decorations,"
said Rosa.

"We need some doggie treats," said Leo.

"We need to make cupcakes for our guests!"
said Libby.

Sprinkles wagged her tail.

She was excited, too.

Libby and Rosa found
the perfect cupcake recipe.
The cupcakes looked fluffy and yummy.
Each cupcake had a candy paw print
on the top.
"These are so cute!" said Rosa.

The friends read the list of ingredients.

"I'll get the sugar, flour, and baking powder," said Libby.

"I'll get the milk, vanilla, and butter," said Rosa.

Leo knocked over
the baking powder
by mistake.
What a mess!
"Leo!" said Libby.

The friends got out mixing bowls,
measuring spoons, and measuring cups.
Libby found the hand mixer.
"Let's bake!" she said.
"Ruff," said Sprinkles.

Libby read the recipe.
"First we need
to measure the flour,"
she said.

Rosa picked up
a measuring cup.
She carefully measured
1 and ½ cups of flour,
then poured it into a bowl.

"What's next?" asked Rosa.

"Now we mix the other ingredients in a different bowl," said Libby.

In a second bowl,

Libby and Rosa mixed together

1 cup of sugar,

½ cup of butter,

2 teaspoons of vanilla,

and 2 eggs.

"Now what does the recipe say?" Rosa asked.

Libby read the directions.

"We have to mix all the ingredients
and then stir in a ½ cup of milk," she said.

"Make sure there are no lumps," said Rosa.

"Mixing is just as important as measuring,"
said Libby.

The friends took turns mixing the batter
until it was perfect.

"That looks good," said Libby.

"Yay, it's time to bake
the cupcakes!"
said Rosa.

Rosa put paper liners into the cupcake pan.

The liners were decorated with paw prints.

Libby spooned batter into each liner.

She filled each liner halfway.

She used only half of
the batter in the bowl.

Libby's mom put the cupcakes into
the oven and set the timer.

"Are they done yet?" Leo asked.

"The recipe says they need to bake
for 20 minutes," Rosa said.

"Let's decorate for the party
while the cupcakes are baking!"
Libby said.

Libby, Leo, and Rosa
strung streamers around the yard.

They set up a doggie grooming station
and a bubble machine.

They set up hoops
to jump through.

They even made
a special
"Happy Birthday"
sign.

Leo poured doggie
treats into bowls.

DING!

"The cupcakes are ready!" Rosa said.

Libby's mom pulled the hot cupcake pan out of the oven.

"Oh, no! Our cupcakes are flat," Libby said.

"And they're hard!" Rosa said.

"They look like rocks!" said Leo.

"They sure aren't fluffy," said Libby.

"What happened?" said Rosa.

Libby noticed the spilled baking powder
on the counter.

"We forgot an important ingredient!"
she said. "Baking powder is what makes
the cupcakes rise."

"Do we have to start over?" asked Rosa.

"I don't think so," Libby said.

"We still have half the batter left."

Libby and Rosa studied the recipe again.
"It says to use 1 and ½ teaspoons
of baking powder," Rosa said.
She reached for the measuring spoon.
"Wait!" said Libby. "We only have
half the batter left, so we should cut
that amount in half."

"Good thinking!" said Rosa.

"What is half of 1 and ½ teaspoons?"

"I know," said Libby.

"It's ¾ of a teaspoon!"

Rosa measured
the baking powder.

Leo mixed
it in with the batter.

Libby's mom put
the new batch of cupcakes
into the oven.

"Cross your fingers!" Libby said.

This time, when the cupcakes came out, they were perfect!

"Yummy!" said Leo.

"Everyone's going to love these," said Rosa.

"We need to decorate them
before our guests get here," Libby said.
"They still need to cool," said Rosa.
"We're running out of time!"
"Ruff!" said Sprinkles.

While they waited, Libby, Rosa, and Leo
stuffed goodie bags for their guests.

Every pup would get
one chew toy
and one doggie treat.

And every friend
would get
a puppy sticker
and a puppy pencil.

Finally, the cupcakes were cool.

Libby, Rosa, and Leo frosted each one.

Then they decorated them
with paw prints made of candy.
They finished just in the nick of time.

Minutes later, the guests arrived.

The humans put on their party hats.

And the pups wore their doggie bandanas.

There was a lot of barking!

There was even more wagging!

The pups played pin the tail on the cat.
Sprinkles won.

The pups played musical mats.
Sprinkles lost.

Some dogs were groomed.

Some dogs took naps.

The pups loved their treats.

And everyone loved the cupcakes.

"How did you make such fluffy cupcakes?"
asked Libby's mom.

"We mixed and measured," said Libby.

"We frosted and decorated," said Leo.

"Baking is so much fun," said Rosa.

"That's because baking is science," said Libby.

"And I love science!"

Libby

LOVES SCIENCE

Having fun with Mix and Measure

Colors (MIX)

When you are making frosting for your cupcakes, mix up different colors.
What happens when you mix pink frosting and blue frosting?
What color frosting do you have now?
What other colors can you mix together?

Cooking and Baking Units (MEASURE)

Gather some measuring cups and measuring spoons. Fill a bowl with water.
How many teaspoons of water fit in a tablespoon?
How many tablespoons of water does it take to fill a cup?
How many cups of water does it take to fill a gallon?

Glossary

Bake: a way to cook food using dry heat

Ingredient: a substance that forms part of a mixture

Mix: making a substance by stirring two or more ingredients together

Measure: determining the size or quantity of something

Mix or measure?

Mix or measure?

Mix or measure?

Mix or measure?

Libby's Puppy Party Cupcakes

(Makes 12 cupcakes)

1 cup white sugar

½ cup softened butter

2 eggs

2 teaspoons vanilla extract

1 ½ cups all-purpose flour

1 ½ teaspoons baking powder

½ cup milk

Preheat oven to 350 degrees F (175 degrees C).
Grease and flour a cupcake pan, or use paper liners.

In a bowl, mix together dry ingredients
(flour and baking powder).

In another bowl, mix together the sugar and butter.
Beat in the eggs, one at a time, then stir in the vanilla.

Add the flour and baking powder mixture
to the wet mixture and mix well.

Finally, stir in the milk until batter is smooth.

Pour or spoon batter into the pan or liners.

Bake 20 to 25 minutes.

Cupcakes are done when they spring back to the touch.
Allow cupcakes to cool, then add frosting.

**Experimenting with science is fun, but remember
that safety comes first, and always make sure
a grown-up is there to help if you need it!**